MATT PHELAN

SWEATER WEATHER

GREENWILLOW BOOKS, *An Imprint of* HarperCollins*Publishers*

FOR NORA AND JASPER

Pencil, ink, and watercolor on hot-pressed paper were used to prepare the full-color art.
The text type is Adobe Caslon Pro.

Library of Congress Cataloging-in-Publication Data

Names: Phelan, Matt, author, illustrator.
Title: Sweater weather / written and illustrated by Matt Phelan.
Description: New York, NY : Greenwillow Books, an imprint of HarperCollins
    Publishers, [2021] | Audience: Ages 4–8. | Audience: Grades K–1. | Summary:
    "On a crisp, fall day and evening, rambunctious bear cubs turn getting dressed
    into an adventure"— Provided by publisher.
Identifiers: LCCN 2021023665 | ISBN 9780062934147 (hardcover)
Subjects: CYAC: Sweaters—Fiction. | Bears—Fiction. | Autumn—Fiction. |
    LCGFT: Picture books.
Classification: LCC PZ7.P44882 Sw 2021 | DDC [E]—dc23
LC record available at https://lccn.loc.gov/2021023665

21 22 23 24 25 RTLO 10 9 8 7 6 5 4 3 2 1
First Edition

Greenwillow Books

NOT YET.

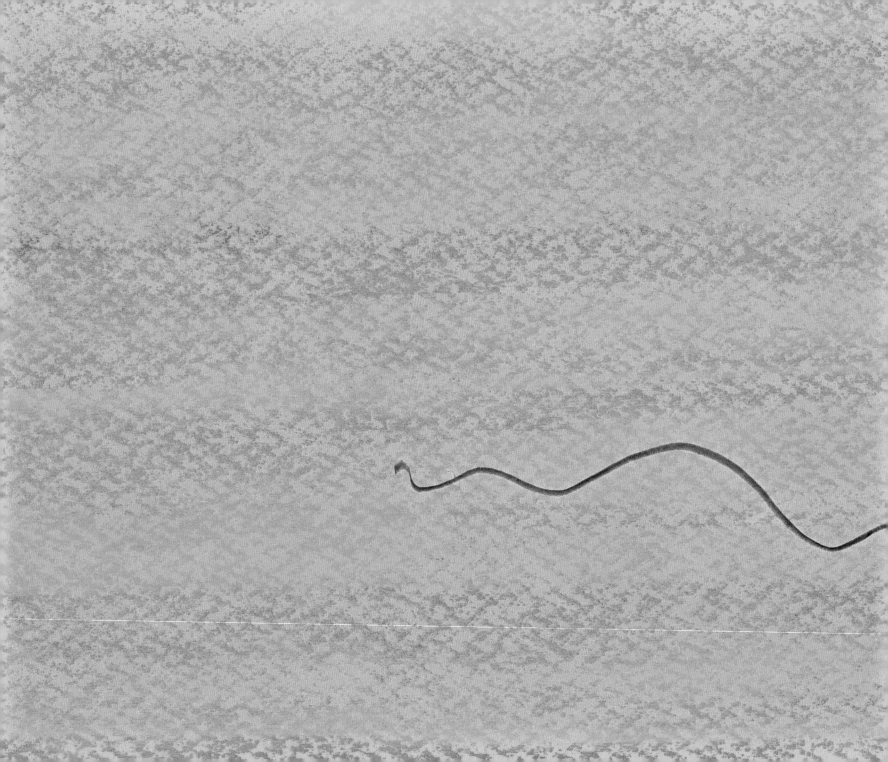